KIDS CAN COPE

Bounce Back from Disappointment

by Gill Hasson

illustrated by Sarah Jennings

Franklin Watts
First published in Great Britain in 2021
by The Watts Publishing Group

Copyright in the text Gill Hasson 2021
Copyright in the illustrations Franklin Watts 2021

Series Editor: Jackie Hamley
Series Designer: Cathryn Gilbert

A CIP catalogue record for this book is
available from the British Library.

ISBN 978 1 4451 6620 9 (hbk)
ISBN 978 1 4451 6619 3 (pbk)

Printed in China

Franklin Watts
An imprint of
Hachette Children's Group
Part of The Watts Publishing Group
Carmelite House
50 Victoria Embankment
London EC4Y 0DZ

An Hachette UK Company
www.hachette.co.uk

www.franklinwatts.co.uk

FSC
www.fsc.org
MIX
Paper from
responsible sources
FSC® C104740

Bounce Back from Disappointment

When things don't happen the way we hoped, we often feel disappointed.

This book can help you deal with those feelings and bounce back from disappointment.

What is disappointment?

Disappointment happens when things don't go the way you thought or hoped that they would. Maybe you've been disappointed when you couldn't go on a school trip because you were unwell.

Perhaps you've been disappointed you missed the bus and had to walk to the shops instead.

Or you were disappointed that you didn't win the game you were playing.

How do you feel?

Disappointment can leave you
feeling sad and upset. It can leave
you feeling let down.

Disappointment can lead to you feeling cross and angry, and feeling that things just aren't fair.

Sometimes, you might just be
a little bit disappointed about something.
But if you were really hoping that something would
happen, or if you've been wanting something for a long
time, then you might feel very disappointed.

What you might do when you're disappointed

Sometimes you might feel disappointed about something for a while, and then you move on and think about or do something else. But there may be times when the disappointed feelings just won't go away.

If you think that someone has let you down, you might feel like you don't want to talk to them or join in with what they're doing.

There may be times when you feel so disappointed that you stop trying to do something and just give up altogether.

What happens when you're stuck in disappointment?

When you're disappointed, it's okay to feel sad and upset, cross and angry, and not want to join in for a while.

But if you stay disappointed for a long time – stuck thinking about what did or didn't happen – that doesn't help you make things better.

Think differently

Rather than staying stuck in disappointment,
it's more helpful if you think about something positive
and imagine things that can happen rather than
thinking about what didn't happen.

When Alba went to watch her favourite football team,
she was disappointed when the team lost the match.
Alba said to herself, "That's the second match
we've lost! We're useless!"

But then she thought, "I'm disappointed with how we played and I wish we had won, but we have two weeks until the next match. There's plenty of time to get better."

Do things differently

When you feel let down and disappointed –
by a situation, by another person, or even by yourself –
focus on what you can do, rather than what you can't do.

Kit belongs to a drama club.
He hoped to get the lead part
acting and singing in the play.
Kit was disappointed when he
forgot his lines, and his teacher
gave the lead part to his friend
Pavlos instead.

But rather than staying disappointed, Kit decided
he was going to learn his lines perfectly for the part
he had been given, and be the very best he could.
He also decided that he wouldn't let this stop him
from trying out for the lead in the next school play.

Say well done to the winners!

Even though you might be disappointed when you don't get what you want or things don't happen the way you hoped, do try and be pleased for others when things work out for them. Congratulate them and say well done. Being nice to others when they do well is a good, positive thing you can do.

You got the lead part; good for you!

Of course, it's not easy to say well done to someone else when you feel disappointed. It can feel even harder to congratulate other people if you are disappointed in yourself – if you messed up or it just didn't go to plan. But you can try! And, because you know what it feels like to be disappointed, next time you know someone else is feeling that way, be kind to them.

Keep on trying!

What else can you do the next time you feel disappointed? Rather than get stuck thinking about what didn't happen, keep on trying!

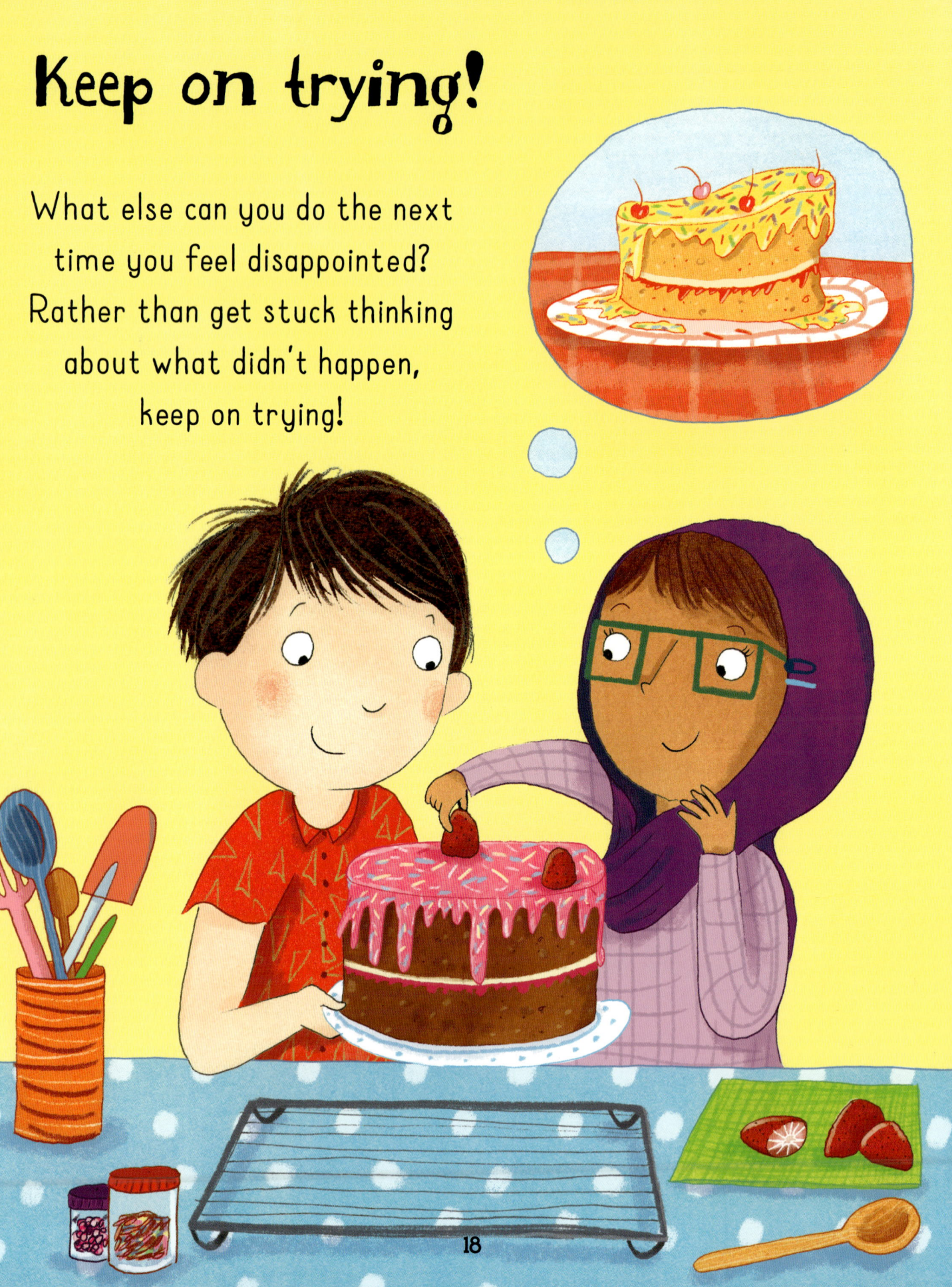

It takes lots of practice to become
good at things – and often you
will struggle and make mistakes.
But if you keep on trying,
you can get better all the time.

William was disappointed
that he didn't do well in the
history test. So William
asked his teacher if
she could help him to
do better next time.

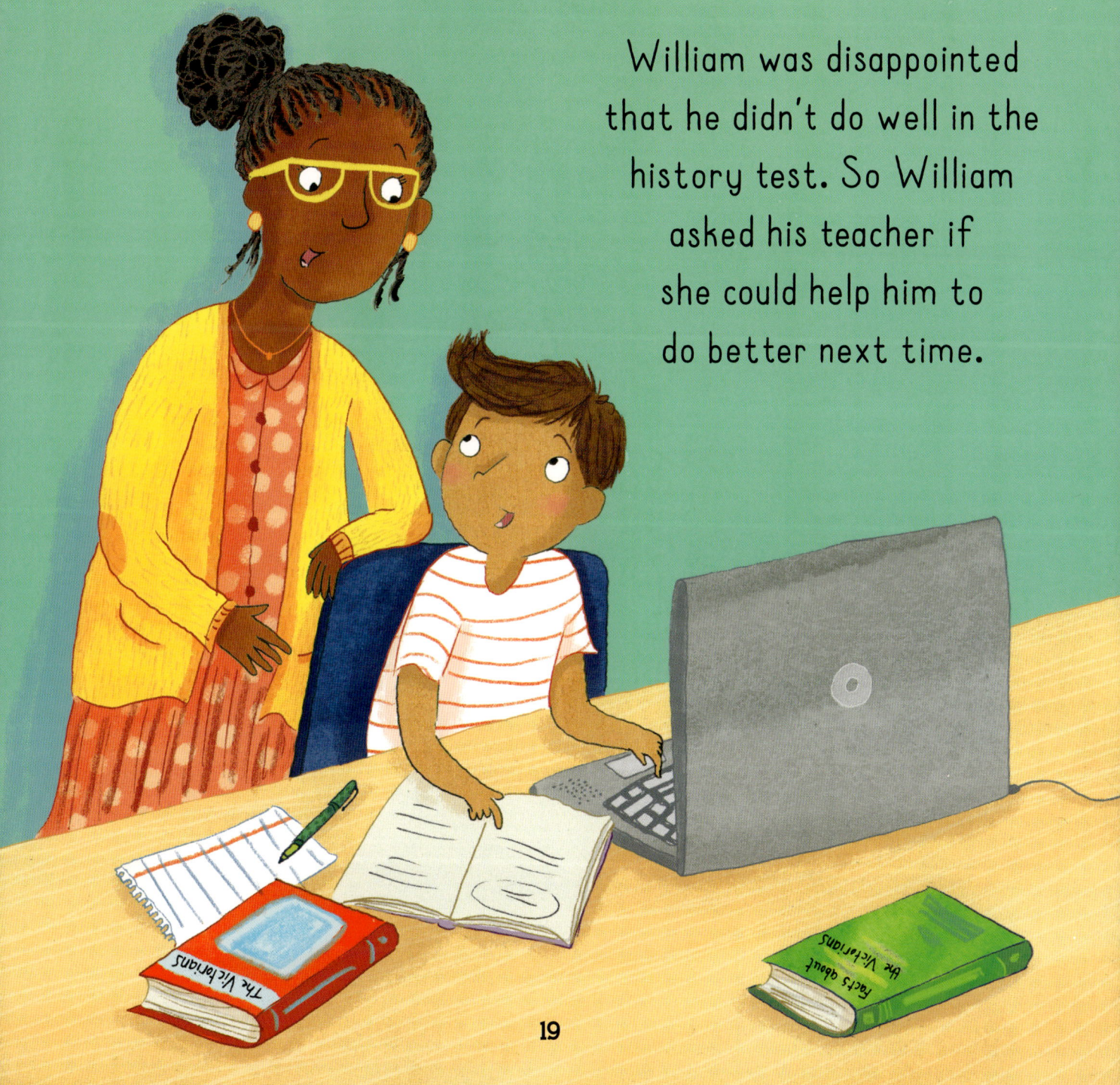

Have a Plan B

In some situations, it can be helpful to think of a Plan B. When you have a Plan B, you have a plan for what to do if what you planned and hoped to do – Plan A – doesn't work out.

Suppose you had planned a party with a picnic in the park. This would be your Plan A. Your Plan B would be a plan for what you would do if, on the day of the party, the weather was cold and wet.

Oh well – it's good that we thought of a Plan B. We'll have the party indoors.

If you've already thought what you'll do if the weather turns bad, you can still have the party!

Feeling let down

Sometimes, there's not much you can do to prevent disappointment. But you can decide how you deal with it.

Someone may tell you that they're going to do something, but then something happens and they're not able to do it. This can leave you feeling disappointed and let down.

Pari's dad said he would take Pari and her brother Tom swimming on Saturday. But on Friday night, he phoned and said he was sorry, but he had to work.

Oh, okay.

Pari and Tom felt really let down. But they didn't want the whole weekend to be spoiled. So Pari said, "Let's ask Mum if we can make a den instead. And we'll ask Dad to find another day we can go swimming with him."

Ask for help

There may be times when you to need to ask a grown-up or a friend to help you move past disappointment. Tell them you're disappointed – you feel sad, upset or angry – and would like some help to think of how to move on from the disappointment. Ask them if they have ever felt disappointed about something, and how they handled it.

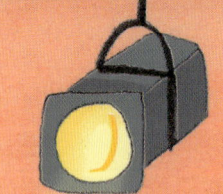

Move on from disappointment

Often, you can be disappointed about things you probably won't even remember in a week's time or in a month's time!

It can help you deal with disappointment if you can tell yourself that, although a disappointment might be difficult right now, it won't be such a big deal soon. Over time, you might even forget all about it!

Karim was upset that his team didn't win the dance competition. But he still loved dancing. He knew that there would be more competitions in the future and that he would still enjoy his dance classes.

Be pleased with what you have

It can also be helpful to think about what you do have and what you can do. So, you might be disappointed that you're not brilliant at running, but perhaps you're good at climbing.

Or maybe you're disappointed that you're not allowed to have a dog, but you do have another pet – perhaps you have a cat, or perhaps your friend has a dog that you can spend time with.

Bounce back from disappointment

Now you know that when you're disappointed, it's okay to feel sad and upset, or cross and angry. But try not to stay stuck in disappointment for too long. There are things you can do to cope with disappointment and feel better. Here's a reminder:

- Think differently. Rather than stay stuck thinking about what didn't happen, think about what could happen next.
- Do things differently. Rather than think about what you can't do, think about what you can do instead.
- Have a Plan B for what you can do in case Plan A doesn't work out.
- Even if you don't do or get what you wanted, do say well done to others.
- And next time you know someone else is disappointed, do be kind to them.

If your disappointment feels too big to handle, ask a grown-up for help. If you don't feel you can ask anyone you know, you can call ChildLine on 0800 1111, or go to www.childline.org.uk to sign up and send an email or post on the message boards. They will listen to you and give you some help and advice about what to do when you're feeling disappointed.

Sometimes, we can't help feeling disappointed.

Now you know how to help yourself bounce back from disappointment!

Activities

These drawing and writing activities can help you to think more about how to deal with disappointment. You could keep your pictures and writing with this book so that you have your own ideas about how to cope when you're disappointed by something.

- Look at yourself in the mirror and make a disappointed face. Draw a picture of it.

- Think of a time you were disappointed about something. What happened when you felt disappointed? What did you think and what did you do? Draw a picture or write about it.

- Then draw or write about how you would deal with it now; now that you've learnt some new ways to deal with disappointment.

- Evie is disappointed because her grandfather is unwell and can't join her family on holiday next week. Write a letter to Evie to help her deal with her disapppointment.

- Simon says that if he doesn't get a ticket for the cricket match next week, he'll be very disappointed. Write a letter to Simon with your idea for a Plan B - what he could do if he doesn't get a ticket - so that he isn't stuck feeing disappointed.

Notes for teachers, parents and carers

Not being invited to a party or offered a place at a school they were hoping to attend, not doing so well at playing a game or a sport, can all be sources of disappointment for a child. So can seeing their team lose, a day out being cancelled, or someone else failing to fulfil a promise they had made. Disappointment happens when things don't go the way we hoped or expected that they would. Just as it can for adults, disappointment can leave a child feeling upset and discouraged, or cross and angry.

When your child is feeling disappointed, your response needs to strike a balance between empathy and understanding, encouragement and problem solving. You need to avoid jumping in with your own solutions or dismissing their disappointment; implying they're overreacting or being silly won't help.

Certainly, disappointment doesn't feel good, but like so many 'negative' emotions, it actually has a positive purpose. Disappointment is an emotion that's rooted in sadness and, like sadness, when we feel disappointed, taking time to sit with it allows us to come to terms with the fact that what has happened has happened and nothing can change that. Your child needs to be able to just sit with their disappointment for a time. However, dwelling for too long on what did or didn't happen keeps them stuck and unable to move past the disappointment.

Children need effective techniques and strategies to help them take control and feel in control. *Bounce Back from Disappointment* explains ways in which your child can do this.

There are a number of strategies to cope with and move on from disappointment, which you can help them with. Having first listened to how they feel about the situation, talk together about what they can do next. How did they handle their last disappointment? What helped? What didn't help? What do they think they could do now? A disappointment gives children the opportunity to learn something — whether about themselves, another person or the situation — and to move forward with what they have learnt.

Although your child can read this book by themselves, it will be more helpful for both of you if you could read it together. Your child might want to read the book in one go. Others will find it easier to manage and understand if they just read a few pages at a time. Either way, there are lots of talking points. Ask your child questions such as: Have you ever tried that? What do you think of that idea? How could that work for you? Talk about the characters in the illustrations.

Having read the book and helped your child identify some strategies that could work for them, you could come back to the book to remind yourselves of the ideas and suggestions for any future disappointment. If something didn't turn out so well, talk together about what they could have done differently. With patience, support and encouragement from you, your child can learn to cope with and better manage disappointment.

If though, you are concerned that your child struggles to cope with and move past disappointments, if they get stuck in negative ways of thinking and are constantly discouraged or angered by disappointments, then it's worth seeking more advice. You can go to youngminds.org.uk or phone their parents' helpline free on 0808 802 5544.